WINTER
COUNT

ALSO BY THE AUTHOR

Desert Notes: Reflections in the Eye of a Raven

Giving Birth to Thunder, Sleeping with His Daughter:
Coyote Builds North America

Of Wolves and Men

River Notes: The Dance of Herons

Barry Holstun Lopez

WINTER COUNT

CHARLES SCRIBNER'S SONS · NEW YORK

"Buffalo" originally appeared in *Chouteau Review* as
"Intentions in North America: The Buffalo." "The Lover
of Words" originally appeared in *North American Review*.

Epigraphs: "Song of Recognition," from *Striking
the Dark Air for Music*, copyright © 1973 William Pitt Root,
used with permission; from the preface to the 1967 edition
of *The Book of Imaginary Beings*, Jorge Luis Borges with
Margarita Guerrero.

The lines recalled by the narrator in "Winter Count 1973: Geese, They
Flew Over in a Storm," from a poem called "Arctic," copyright © 1977
William Pitt Root, are scanned

> to hunch and spread
> his wings and tail and fall
> silent as moonlight
> upon the quick hot
> frenzy in that fur.

and are used with the permission of *The Nation*.

Library of Congress Cataloging in Publication Data

Lopez, Barry Holstun, 1945–
  Winter count.

  CONTENTS: Restoration.—Winter herons.—Buffalo.—
[etc.]
  I. Title.
PS3562.067W5   1981   813'.54   80–29454
ISBN 0–684–16817–0

1 3 5 7 9 11 13 15 17 19 Q/C 20 18 16 14 12 10 8 6 4 2

Printed in the United States of America

Illustrations copyright © 1981 Ted Lewin

Book design by Joel Schick

For Friends,

Their Uncommon Grace

Contents

Restoration   1

Winter Herons   15

Buffalo   27

The Orrery   37

Winter Count 1973:
Geese, They Flew Over in a Storm   51

The Tapestry   65

The Woman Who Had Shells   77

The Lover of Words   87

The Location of the River   99

After the long letters
have been written, read,
abandoned, after
distances grow absolute
and speech, too,
is distance, only
listening is left.

I have heard the dark hearts
of the stones
that beat once in a lifetime.

WILLIAM PITT ROOT

We are ignorant of the meaning of the dragon
in the same way that we are ignorant of the
meaning of the universe, but there is something
in the dragon's image that fits man's imagination,
and this accounts for the dragon's appearance in
different places and periods.

JORGE LUIS BORGES

Among several tribes on the northern plains,
the passage of time from one summer to the next
was marked by noting a single memorable event.
The sequence of such memories, recorded
pictographically on a buffalo robe or spoken aloud,
was called a winter count.
Several winter counts might be in progress
at any one time in the same tribe, each differing
according to the personality of its keeper.

Restoration

J UST OVER the Montana border in North Dakota, north of the small town of Killdeer, there is a French mansion. It is part of a frontier estate built in 1863 for a titled family called de Crenir, from Bordeaux. When the last of the de Crenirs died in France in 1904, the two-story Victorian house, its contents, and the surrounding acres were bequeathed to the nearby town. Looking incongruous still in the vast landscape of brown hills, it has since stood as a tourist attraction.

There are various explanations for why the house

was built in such a desolate place, after the fur trade had passed on but before the Indian wars were over and settlement had come. In time, the Great Northern Railroad reached it, but the first de Crenirs had to come up by boat seven hundred miles from St. Louis and finish the journey by horse. According to a pamphlet given to tourists, the family had had thoughts of establishing a cattle empire, but their visits were irregular and short. In spite of the rich furnishings freighted in and installed and the considerable expense and trouble involved in construction, only one, René de Crenir, ever overwintered there. His visits began in the spring of 1883 and he arrived each spring thereafter, departing each fall until he took up permanent residence in 1887. Seven years later, in the summer of 1894, he left abruptly, and no de Crenir ever came again. This young de Crenir, too, the pamphlet goes on to say, was the only one of the family to visit regularly with people in town, or who rode more than a day's journey into the surrounding country.

The gray and white house gives the impression now of being a military outpost on the edge of an empire of silence and space, the domain, at the time it was built, of buffalo, bear, antelope, wolves, Hunkpapa Sioux, Crows off to the west, and others. Today there is little of value left beyond the house itself and a few pieces of period furniture except a collection of extraordinary books.

In the summer of 1974, this collection was in the

4

process of being restored by a man named Edward Seraut. I was driving east and saw a highway advertisement outside Killdeer—HISTORIC FRENCH CHATEAU • 12 MILES • ICE CREAM • COOL DRINKS • SOUVENIRS—and had stopped and toured the mansion with other people on vacation. Afterward, with a guard's permission and anticipating a conversation, I went back to the library on the second floor and introduced myself, somewhat hesitantly, to Seraut.

I had been struck right away by the sight of him, sitting still and jacketless in a straight chair with a broken book in his lap, as though bereaved. He was perhaps in his sixties. He seemed gratified by my interest, though I startled him when I came up. He showed me, still with a slightly quizzical look, a few of the books he had been working on—an oversized folio of colored prints of North American mammals by Karl Bodmer, and a copy, I recognized, of La Mettrie's *L'Homme Machine*. He described a technique he was just then using to remove a stain called foxing from a flyleaf. I was drawn to him. When I asked if I might take him to dinner, he said he would be glad—delighted.

"I've been here for months," he said, "and I've hardly looked out the windows."

While I waited for the estate to close—Seraut said he was obliged to work in public view until closing time—I walked out into the surrounding hills. They had a smoothness of line, an evenness of tone, that is often called graceful, the sun-dried grasses being everywhere the same height. I wondered if these might be the native grasses, come back. The dry hills seemed without life, though in the distance, through shimmering heat waves, some Herefords or other kind of cattle were grazing.

When I returned to the house, Seraut was not quite ready and, glad to watch, I insisted he go on. His tools appeared surgical. Laid out on a long refectory table, amid presses and rolls of paper and leather, were forceps and scalpels, tweezers, syringes filled with glue, many spools of thread and several kinds of knives. The room was filled, too, with a pleasing light, but when I remarked about it, Seraut said this was one of the reasons the collection had deteriorated—that, and the fact that many of the books had been so heavily used. He indicated the worn headband on a book as he handed it to me. I knew this book, too, William Bartram's *Travels Through North and South Carolina*—a first edition. But I was mesmerized more by Seraut's efficiency. He had beveled a frayed corner clean and then anchored a new piece of book board to it with tiny steel pins, like a bone fracture. When he covered the corner with leather, the matching of line and texture was so deft the repair seemed never to have been made. Indeed, like the other corners, it appeared slightly rubbed from use.

He firmed the book in a small press and we left.

*

On the way into town we both marveled at the broad reach, the sultry reds and oranges, the lingering yellows, of the North Dakota sunset. Seraut remarked on the fine shading of colors, their densities. Leathers, he said, after a moment, could be treated with certain vegetable dyes to achieve a range of color as subtle. I asked, did one, in taking advantage of such skills, restore a book so well it avoided detection? Or did one leave clear evidence of what had been done, so as not to confuse the issue of originality? He leaned toward the former, he said, but always tipped a small sheet of paper into the back of the book, noting the date of restoration and what he had done.

I had been attracted to Seraut because of his work, and the atmosphere of well-read books; but there was a kind of incongruity about him, too, that was as attractive. His dress was foreign, a dark wool suit, a white shirt with a plain dark tie. He was mannered—a suggestion of polite intentions and cultivated tastes. There was almost the air of a prior about him. He seemed oblivious to the country in which he was now at work.

He had been hired, he told me, by a man in Illinois, a lawyer who had bought the de Crenir collection. A committee of townspeople had advertised it for sale in order to raise money to refurbish the mansion—629 leather-bound volumes belonging to René de Crenir, most on topics of natural history, some dating from the sixteenth century. The man had asked Seraut to travel to North Dakota, to restore the collection and prepare it for shipment east.

Seraut said he spent his days filling insect holes, repairing deteriorating spines, restoring gold tooling—"accurate and sympathetic restoration," he told me, "not crude mutilations or the inappropriate embellishments of amateurs." If necessary he would dismantle a book entirely in order to resize and rehinge each page, before sewing it all back together. He had been working for three months but would need another few weeks, he thought, to finish. He lived at the de Crenir mansion. He said nothing of any contact with the townspeople. The afternoon I met him he had paid no attention at all to the tourists who had wandered through.

Over dinner, perhaps because of the wine, he spoke with sudden passion of the art and obscurity of his profession, at one point emphasizing the obscurity with a gesture of his arm toward the far reaches of the prairie that lay beyond the walls of the hotel. I tried to listen politely but was caught by an offhand reference to being able to reconstruct René de Crenir's intellectual life, through a study of the collection. How? I asked.

The volumes that have seen the most use, he went on, indicated de Crenir's principal concern was with the presence of animals in North America that were unknown in Europe. The library contained first editions of the journals and letters of James Oglethorpe, Thomas Nuttall, André Michaux, and Cadwallader Colden, all of whom were among the earliest to make extensive, first-hand notes on the natural history of North America. There were copies, too, of many of the early accounts of plains exploration—Lewis and Clark, Bradbury, Stewart. Seraut said he believed de Crenir had been *obsessed* with understanding the nature of animals foreign to the European mind, that he wanted a *new* understanding, rooted in North America and representing a radically different view of the place of animals in human ideas.

To want to try to do this, I said, was certainly reasonable. European naturalists had groped at first for European analogs to describe unfamiliar animals— they had referred to American coyotes, for example, as jackals. The stories of alligators and eight-foot diamondback rattlesnakes they brought home were not taken seriously, nor was the idea that a grizzly bear might not be fazed by three or four bullets. The soulless vision of creatures set forth at the time by Descartes and Linnaeus was not affected by the North American discoveries and it soon absorbed them, passing right over the native taxonomies. De Crenir, I said, may have wanted to throw out the European system and fit the American animals to a new system—but how?

We ordered brandy and cigars after dinner. I was

now deeply affected by the atmosphere of ideas and history that emanated from Seraut, and periodically stunned by the sight of young, ferine men cruising in slow-moving pickups on the other side of the window, or distracted by the rise and fall of ranchers' voices and the din of country-and-western music in an adjoining bar. As Seraut speculated, I became more and more fascinated by de Crenir. Had he ever published? Seraut shrugged. Perhaps, but he thought not. There were only stray notes, no manuscripts. Risking the feeling of camaraderie, I asked if I could examine the library the next day. I knew some natural history; perhaps I could construct an outline of de Crenir's work. Seraut said he had no objection, though I sensed he thought my interest precipitate and improper.

I drove him back. In the August moonlight, the North Dakota hills appeared in soft outline, gentle and unearthly.

By the time I arrived the next morning the first visitors had already been through. Seraut was at work in shirt sleeves. Not wishing to disturb him, I began to read the titles of books on the shelves, examining a few at random as I went along. One I pulled down, on the classification of European butterflies, was interspersed with thin sheets of paper on which were written notes in French—I assumed in René de Crenir's hand— about Hermes, Atalanta, and others from Greek mythology. Similar notes in other books referred to the Eddas, the *Bhagavad-Gita*. Those books not concerned with natural history bore mostly on religion, philosophy, and Catholic theology.

Underneath a pair of tall casement windows there was an empty table. With an enquiring nod to Seraut, who looked up expressionless from what he was doing, I laid out several volumes and began to make notes of my own. I worked through a long morning, looking away occasionally only to study the older man. His fingers were crooked slightly with arthritis but moved deliberately and adroitly over his materials. In the bright sunlight slanting into the high-ceilinged room the thin skin of his forearms appeared glassine. He seemed, even in this library, an anachronism.

From what I could discover, de Crenir was an anti-rationalist, at odds with the Age of Reason, a champion of Montaigne. Once or twice I engaged Seraut in conversation, briefly sharing my ideas and enthusiasm. He directed me to other volumes; though he was taken up with its restoration, his interest in the contents of the collection seemed as intent. From these titles, their chapters and marginal notes, I gleaned that de Crenir believed a cultural and philosophic bias had prevented nineteenth-century European naturalists from comprehending much of the plant and animal life they saw in North America. The resulting confusion, he believed, had kept them in ignorance of something even more profound: de Crenir had written in the margin of Maximilian's *Reise in das innere Nord-Amerika,* "Ici les bêtes sont les propriétaires"—in North America the indigenous philosophy grew out of the lives of animals.

De Crenir was largely correct—as subsequent work by anthropologists made clear. What was so startling was that in the whole of his library there were only eight or ten books that bore in any way at all on native American philosophy, only such things as the works of James Hall. De Crenir had apparently reached these conclusions alone.

From here, I did not know where to go. If de Crenir thought animals the owners of the landscape, or even, in theological terms, equal with men, whom might he have spoken with about it? Whom had he written?

Mr. Seraut and I had a late lunch together by one of the large windows. He seemed pleased by my findings. I said, out of a rush of ideas, that I might work on here for several days if that was all right and then possibly contact a friend who spoke excellent French. He showed me a book he had just taken out of the press. When I hesitated to hold it because of its beauty, he urged me to take it, to listen to the rattle of its pages, to examine the retooling. When he took the book back he said he preferred the older traditions. Where gold tooling was now restored with the aid of shellacs, he still used egg whites and vinegar, as had been done for four hundred years. His glues were still made from wheat flour. They would outlast the paper in some of the books.

I asked him over our sandwiches if he had ever read any of Montaigne. Oh yes. Once, in Leningrad, he had restored a bound collection of Montaigne's letters. He had read Montaigne's misgivings about his work in his own hand. He spoke in a genial way, as though misgivings were a part of everything.

Out the window we could see several miles across the rolling brown hills. In a draw below the house there suddenly appeared six antelope, frozen so still they seemed to shimmer in the dry grass. I saw sunlight glinting on the surface of their huge eyes, their hearts beating against soft, cream-white throats, the slender legs. Surprised by the house, or by us in the window, they were as suddenly gone. At the end of the room, beyond a blue velvet rope strung between polished brass stanchions, a line of tourists passed. They stared at us and then looked away nervously into the shelves of books. A girl in yellow shorts was eating ice cream. In a shaft of window light I could see the wheat paste dried to granules under Seraut's fingernails and the excessive neatness of my own notes, the black ink like a skittering of shore birds over the white sheets.

Winter Herons

HE KNEW that the azure blue skies above New York in October, the unassailable purity of the color, could release tears in him if he watched long enough. Seated on black marble, its darkness cool under his palms, the stone itself racketed as he looked deeper with ganglia of white neurons, he imagined he stood alone farther north, as in a Sung painting; stood beneath black skies with the white heartbeat of stars overhead and that rip tide of light, that Tai-chi extension of otherly grace, the northern lights.

"I have no idea," he had told her once, "why I long to be in that landscape, but I do. Maybe it is only being alone, infinitesimal. I can look at a whimbrel, the long-legged, hesitating movement, as if the bird were waiting for thoughts to enter its mind, and understand why in that vast tundra it chooses as it does precisely one lonely place to sit."

She had smiled at him. She knew he was right. She had never heard of a whimbrel.

In the faces that moved past him now, over the purling of footsteps, he saw distortion, greed, subterfuge—predatory expressions; but more often he saw veiled faces, passing quick as sparrows or deer, unrevealed. In eyes, gray and brown and green, whose averting he caused with his staring, he felt affability just out of reach. He did not think there was more distrust here than on the streets of other cities, as he had always heard. More tension, perhaps. He regarded his shadow breaking up in the clothing of passersby, the sun coming over his shoulder down the long corridor of a crosstown street. Then the fandango of bright skirts and trousers parted, like a sudden upwelling of wood ducks, and the shadow of him rung on the sidewalk like the gnomen of a sundial.

He had asked her to go north with him in June, when the light would hang over the land in unending compassion, when evenings were cool, before the mosquitoes came—at one in the morning the sky would still be too bright to hold stars; and she had arrived at the airport, the tiny airport, on a flight from Denver, and they had driven out to his aunt's ranch to stay the week before going up.

"And what do you do when you are not dancing?" his aunt had asked.

"I think about dancing!" she burst out, as if for the first time in years she could speak without fear of repercussion. "I think of dances, my head is full of dances!" Then she brought her napkin to her lips, slightly embarrassed.

He smiled into his plate, contorted inside with his own ebullience, and said nothing.

They had made love that afternoon beneath cottonwoods, whose leaves swirled and roared in the wind above them, and later, as if the day had detached itself and them from the passage of time, they watched a flight of cranes lumbering over the short grasses into the distant gray-blue skies of Canada.

She did not go with him. It frightened her too much, she said, this unending sky. (He remembered the first time he had seen her dance at the Metropolitan Opera House, the arch of the proscenium so high that no movement onstage could carry the eye to it.) And she said almost whispering that she was afraid she would find nothing to hold her mind, that she was different from him. He watched her out of a powerful singularity from the center of the bedroom, and then he flowed again so he seemed as she always remembered him, generous and surrounded by a haunting reverence.

They rode in the hills around the ranch for three days. He thought of the elk he had killed the year before, wrapped carefully in brown butcher paper in the freezer; he couldn't trust the relationship that far, he thought. He filled her hair with Indian paintbrush and told her that when he was a boy he had ridden a Galapagos tortoise at the San Diego Zoo, that years later it had occurred to him the tortoise could have been more than a hundred and twenty, could have seen the *Beagle* at anchor, watched cow-eyed as Darwin approached over the rocky shore. The only way to have told how old it was would have been to kill it.

The sunlight seemed to tighten his jacket across his shoulders. They rode across the hayfields and she could not stand the thought of leaving, or staying on without making a change that eluded her.

He had gone with her mother once to lunch at a French restaurant in the east eighties. The graciousness of everyone there, that there were only four tables, and the thick linen napkin and the simple food pleased him. Her mother was very fond of him. His education, his teaching, his ingenuous inquisitiveness all undermined her fear that he was without ambition, that he might inherit a ranch in Montana and never leave it. She realized as she watched him, as he unraveled a story she was not listening to, that she loved him because there was nothing in him that awakened memories of her husband. Other men had done that. It was like the sound of mice running across a hardwood floor in the middle of the night.

He looked up at the green glass and aluminum wall that rose sheer for two hundred feet above the words BANK OF JAPAN, fading sunlight rattling weakly on the aluminum, the green like a river, impenetrable as jade. His father was a breaker of horses, who had died of cancer from smoking, a kind of stupidity that made him sit suddenly erect and turn away from the building and look at the people again. He wished to touch their clothing with the tips of his fingers—burnished silk, coarse tweed, ribbed wool; burgundy, gray-brown, deep blue. Pass your hands over winter wheat heading up, lay them flat against the rough bark of an ash tree. The night his father had died he had broken his right hand punching a board in the dark barn where only baled hay should have been.

He'd gotten lost like this before, he thought. The memory of his father was like a ground fog that would not quit him. He looked down the dimming avenue to the Helmsley Building, to the baroque announcement, the distant, resolute, autocratic hands: 6 : 15. He had told her six.

They had gone to a party once, after a performance of *Les Sylphides*. He had met a man there, a choreographer who had studied with Balanchine, who wore half-glasses over which he stared as if in anticipation of directions. He asked the man, had he ever seen sandhill cranes dance? No, why would one? He tried to explain with hands and arms and head, a contained display, how it worked. The man asked, what other birds do this? "Grebes. I have a friend who is filming the mating of grebes, then he will choreograph the movement for friends, a company." Remarkable. He could find no entry with him and wanted to get away quickly. He told him about fishing for cutthroat trout in the headwaters of the Yellowstone, and hated himself for having given grebes to the man.

The hum and click of electric switches in a drab traffic box on the corner carried eerily over the sounds of cars, as if there were strata of sound, some of which had evaporated and left silence, and others that did not penetrate each other. He studied the land sloping away to the west toward the Hudson River, and to the south and it seemed relinquished, covered over with buildings. He wondered what creeks once slipped here, what pines had sighed on such fall evenings. He thought of lines from somewhere in the journals of Kosai, traveling among the Ainu, the very same colors of this image before him, severely muted greens, silver of moonlit water beneath white high clouds; but Kosai's haiku was lost to him in a way he found frightening.

Once, the same summer they were going to go to

the Romanzof Mountains and camp in the ethereal light among nesting plovers and horned larks, watch caribou calve and rough-legged hawks hover in the wind, he had taken her to an island in the Sagebow River. The first night he had ever slept out alone had been on this island. That day she stood at the river's edge with her arms folded across her bare chest looking down the river with a chin line hard enough for that country. She had tied a flicker's feathers in her hair.

The marble had lost its warmth. He stood up and aligned his boots carefully with the sidewalk's hatching. Even in this city you could tell, he thought: frozen creeks, snow, gray mornings—strands of all that were in the wind. You would know putting your face into it, remembering as well as a harvest mouse, perhaps even salmon.

One winter evening in New York he had had dinner with a classmate from Amherst, on 56th Street. When they emerged it was to find it had been snowing. They were dressed for it. They were full of food and wine and did not care to get away anywhere. They stood on the corner of 54th and Park and talked. The falling snow obliterated their footprints and left them standing in a field of white illuminated by a street lamp before the friend finally caught a cab uptown. He watched the cab until it was only red taillights. He did not want to hurry away. In the chilled air and falling snow was some universal forgiveness and he did not want to disturb it. He stepped slowly off the curb, headed south.

Overhead, above the surface of the pool of light cast by the street lamps, the canyon of the wide avenue disappeared into darkness. He had walked only a few blocks when he realized that birds were falling. Great blue herons were descending slowly against the braking of their wings, their ebony legs extended to test the depth of the snow which lay in a garden that divided the avenue. He stood transfixed as the birds settled. They folded their wings and began to mill in the gently falling snow and the pale light. They had landed as if on a prairie, and if they made any sound he did not hear. One pushed its long bill into the white ground. After a moment they were all still. They gazed at the front of a hotel, where someone had just gone through a revolving door. A cab slowed in front of him—he shook his head, no, no, and it went on. One or two of the birds flared their wings to lay off the snow and a flapping suddenly erupted among them and they were in the air again. Fifteen or twenty, flying past with heavy, hushing beats, north up the avenue for two or three blocks before they broke through the plane of light and disappeared.

He walked over to the hotel thinking he would call his friend, but didn't. He walked almost six miles to the tip of the island, where falling snow was melting on the surface of the harbor.

*

The stone beneath his feet was cold and dry. No birds this evening, he thought. He looked at the Helmsley clock: five minutes to seven. The young ginkgo trees spaced so evenly along the edge of the avenue seemed like prisoners to him, indentured ten thousand miles from China.

When he saw her walking slowly with her mother and someone else, it was a little after seven. He wondered if he had said seven, if that's what he had said.

Buffalo

IN JANUARY 1845, after a week of cold but brilliantly clear weather, it began to snow in southern Wyoming. Snow accumulated on the flat in a dead calm to a depth of four feet in only a few days. The day following the storm was breezy and warm—chinook weather. A party of Cheyenne camped in a river bottom spent the day tramping the snow down, felling cottonwood trees for their horses, and securing game, in response to a dream by one of them, a thirty-year-old man called Blue Feather on the Side of His Head, that they would be trapped by a sudden freeze.

That evening the temperature fell fifty degrees and

an ice crust as rigid, as easily broken, as sharp as window glass formed over the snow. The crust held for weeks.

Access across the pane of ice to game and pasturage on the clear, wind-blown slopes of the adjacent Medicine Bow Mountains was impossible for both Indian hunters and a buffalo herd trapped nearby. The buffalo, exhausted from digging in the deep snow, went to their knees by the thousands, their legs slashed by the razor ice, glistening red in the bright sunlight. Their woolly carcasses lay scattered like black boulders over the blinding white of the prairie, connected by a thin crosshatching of bloody red trails.

Winds moaned for days in the thick fur of the dead and dying buffalo, broken by the agonized bellows of the animals themselves. Coyotes would not draw near. The Cheyenne camped in the river bottom were terrified. As soon as they were able to move they departed. No Cheyenne ever camped there again.

The following summer the storm and the death of the herd were depicted on a buffalo robe by one of the Cheyenne, a man called Raven on His Back. Above the scene, in the sky, he drew a white buffalo. The day they had left camp a man was supposed to have seen a small herd of buffalo, fewer than twenty, leaving the plains and lumbering up the Medicine Bow River into the mountains. He said they were all white, and each seemed to him larger than any bull he had ever seen. There is no record of this man's name, but another

Cheyenne in the party, a medicine man called Walks
Toward the Two Rivers, carried the story of the surviv-
ing white buffalo to Crow and Teton Sioux in an effort
to learn its meaning. In spite of the enmity among
these tribes their leaders agreed that the incident was a
common and disturbing augury. They gathered on the
Box Elder River in southeastern Montana in the spring
of 1846 to decipher its meaning. No one was able to
plumb it, though many had fasted and bathed in prep-
aration.

Buffalo were never seen again on the Laramie
Plains after 1845, in spite of the richness of the grasses
there and the size of the buffalo herds nearby in those
days. The belief that there were still buffalo in the
Medicine Bow Mountains, however, survivors of the
storm, persisted for years, long after the disappearance
of buffalo (some 60 million animals) from Wyoming
and neighboring territories by the 1880s.

In the closing years of the nineteenth century,
Arapaho and Shoshoni warriors who went into the
Medicine Bow to dream say they did, indeed, see buffalo up there then. The animals lived among the barren rocks above timberline, far from any vegetation.
They stood more than eight feet at the shoulder; their
coats were white as winter ermine and their huge eyes
were light blue. At the approach of men they would
perch motionless on the granite boulders, like mountain goats. Since fogs are common in these high valleys

in spring and summer it was impossible, they say, to tell how many buffalo there were.

In May 1887 a Shoshoni called Long Otter came on two of these buffalo in the Snowy Range. As he watched they watched him. They began raising and lowering their hooves, started drumming softly on the rocks. They began singing a death song, way back in the throat like the sound of wind moaning in a canyon. The man, Long Otter, later lost his mind and was killed in a buckboard accident the following year. As far as I know this is the last report of living buffalo in the Medicine Bow.

It is curious to me that in view of the value of the hides no white man ever tried to find and kill one of these buffalo. But that is the case. No detail of the terrible storm of that winter, or of the presence of a herd of enormous white buffalo in the Medicine Bow, has ever been found among the papers of whites who lived in the area or who might have passed through in the years following.

It should be noted, however, by way of verification, that a geology student from Illinois called Fritiof Fryxell came upon two buffalo skeletons in the Snowy Range in the summer of 1925. Thinking these barren heights an extraordinary elevation at which to find buffalo, he carefully marked the location on a topographic map. He measured the largest of the skeletons, found the size staggering, and later wrote up the incident in the May 1926 issue of the *Journal of Mammalogy*.

In 1955, a related incident came to light. In the fall of 1911, at the request of the Colorado Mountain Club, a party of Arapaho Indians were brought into the Rocky Mountains in the northern part of the state to relate to white residents the history of the area prior to 1859. The settlers were concerned that during the years when the white man was moving into the area, and the Indian was being extirpated, a conflict in historical records arose such that the white record was incomplete and possibly in error.

The Arapaho were at first reluctant to speak; they made up stories of the sort they believed the whites would like to hear. But the interest and persistence of the white listeners made an impression upon them and they began to tell what had really happened.

Among the incidents the Arapaho revealed was that in the winter of 1845 (when news of white settlers coming in covered wagons first reached them) there was a terrible storm. A herd of buffalo wintering in Brainard Valley (called then Bear in the Hole Valley) began singing a death song. At first it was barely audible, and it was believed the wind was making the sound until it got louder and more distinct. As the snow got deeper the buffalo left the valley and began to climb into the mountains. For four days they climbed, still singing the moaning death song, followed by Arapaho warriors, until they reached the top of the mountain. This was the highest place but it had no name. Now it is called Thatchtop Mountain.

During the time the buffalo climbed they did not stop singing. They turned red all over; their eyes became smooth white. The singing became louder. It sounded like thunder that would not stop. Everyone who heard it, even people four or five days' journey away, was terrified.

At the top of the mountain the buffalo stopped singing. They stood motionless in the snow, the wind blowing clouds around them. The Arapaho men who had followed had not eaten for four days. One, wandering into the clouds with his hands outstretched and a rawhide string connecting him to the others, grabbed hold of one of the buffalo and killed it. The remaining buffalo disappeared into the clouds; the death song began again, very softly, and remained behind them. The wind was like the singing of the buffalo. When the clouds cleared the men went down the mountain.

The white people at the 1911 meeting said they did not understand the purpose of telling such a story. The Arapaho said this was the first time the buffalo tried to show them how to climb out through the sky.

The notes of this meeting in 1911 have been lost, but what happened there remained clear in the mind of the son of one of the Indians who was present. It was brought to my attention by accident one evening in the library of the university where I teach. I was reading an article on the introduction of fallow deer in Nebraska in the August 1955 issue of the *Journal of Mammalogy* when this man, who was apparently just walking by, stopped and, pointing at the opposite page, said, "This is not what this is about." The article he indicated was called "An Altitudinal Record for Bison in Northern Colorado." He spoke briefly of it, as if to himself, and then departed.

Excited by this encounter I began to research the incident. I have been able to verify what I have written here. In view of the similarity between the events in the Medicine Bow and those in Colorado, I suspect that there were others in the winter of 1845 who began, as the Arapaho believe, trying to get away from what was coming, and that subsequent attention to this phenomenon is of some importance.

I recently slept among weathered cottonwoods on the Laramie Plains in the vicinity of the Medicine Bow Mountains. I awoke in the morning to find my legs broken.

The Orrery

NORTH of Tucson and east, beyond Steadman, is a place hardly accessible by car called The Fields. I do not know how it came by this name. I was told by someone, a lifelong resident, that the name grew up after an attempt to irrigate and sell some of the land had failed, that the reference was cynical. The person who tried to sell the land was from Chicago, he said. I think I was told this because I seemed to be traveling through.

The valley is called Tifton on USGS maps. It is flat and dry, covered with creosote bush and ocotillo.

Along the washes are a few deep-rooted paloverde and mesquite trees and, very occasionally in a damp draw, there is a Frémont cottonwood. Tall saguaro cactus are thinly scattered. Closer to the ground are primrose and sand verbena. The brittle soil is a reddish-brown mixture of clays and dry, sedimentary debris. The effect, looking across the valley into the surrounding barren mountains, is bleak, foreboding. In spite of this, I remember the valley by the first name I heard, The Fields, and think of a field of alfalfa like ocean water with the wind rolling over it. Crawling through green, wind-blown alfalfa is one of the earliest memories of my childhood.

I came here first in 1956 on a trip with my father, who was an amateur horticulturist. He was looking for a kind of cactus he had deduced from someone's anthropological notes was growing here. (He found it and it was later named for him: *Cephalocerus greystonii*.) What I remember most from the first visit, however, was neither the dryness nor the cactus but the wind. When I was a child in California the Santa Ana winds that came west to us from this side of the mountains seemed to me exotic but aloof. The wind I found in this upper Sonoran country with my father was very different. It was intoxicating. The wind had a quality of wild refinement about it, like horses turning around suddenly in the air by your ear. Whether it blew steadily or in bursts its strength seemed so evenly to diminish as you turned your face to it, it was as though someone had exhaled through silk. I have never since felt so enticed or comforted by the simple movement of air.

I returned to this valley in 1967 with a friend (whom I would bury the next year in Mexico when a road washed away from under us and left us rolling over crazily in a flash flood). The winds again held me in sway, seemingly alive, so much so that I felt contrite for not having visited in so long. Unable to sleep, I rose several times in the night to smoke a cigarette and, by turning my head slightly one way or the other, to listen. My friend only shrugged his shoulders as I explained, but he made no disparaging remark.

On this same trip I met a man who lived at the western end of the valley, in a small adobe house at the confluence of the dry creeks of Blue and Willow Divide canyons. The first time I saw him he was sweeping a large area of the desert with a broom. As there was no vegetation where he swept, all he could be doing was removing small bits of rock and loose soil. I watched him from behind creosote bushes until some quality of dance or music in his sweeping finally brought me out. I remained concerned as I walked toward him that he might be adrift in another world. My father had told me never to approach such men.

He was pleasant enough, but I could soon see I was imposing somehow. He stopped working while I stood there and did not encourage the conversation. I finally gave an excuse and left. All the way back to the tent I wondered at the improbability and awkwardness of this meeting, feeling that I had ruined something. When my companion returned from a trip to Steadman I told him what had happened. He thought perhaps the man only wanted to be left alone, that I shouldn't have intruded.

As I thought about watching him from the bushes, I thought how most of us come so late to understanding any need for privacy. I had even asked the man why he was sweeping the desert floor. He said it was an opportunity—an impossible task at which to work each day, as one might meditate or pray. He said he lived on land passed down with his family, that he mostly read—Bernal Diaz, when I asked, the volumes of Bernardino de Sahagún on the Aztec, as they became available, Copernicus—and he said he did not mind the loneliness. Several times a year he went to Steadman. Occasionally he would go on to Tucson, where he had grown up but had not been in a while. I understood him to mean the town had lost its heart, as a place that is photographed too much ceases to seem real.

I returned to the valley in 1973, alone, and—to put it honestly—driven. I wanted to see him again. In my memory his grip, even of what little of his life I had seen that day—the rhythmic sweeping, the distant house and garden shaded under mesquite and palo-verde—his grip seemed sure, as though whatever it was he was doing was as good as one might hope to do.

The first evening in the valley I camped by myself and slept hardly at all for the breezes that came and stayed the night. The following morning I walked from the end of the bad road to his house, not more than a mile around the sweeping point of a high, chalky bluff. I noticed as I approached the arbor that sheltered his home that the area he had been sweeping that day was now covered with thousands of stones, seemingly without pattern, though it was impossible to miss the intent of a design.

It was late in the fall, very pleasant weather if you are not used to the heat. He was at home—he remembered me and said I should stay for lunch, if I wished. I experienced a relief at this moment I could not have anticipated. He had just baked bread. There was celery and lettuce from his garden and a kind of small melon I didn't know. Its cool, yellow flesh reminded me instantly of boyhood days in California. When I said this impulsively he raised his spoon and eyebrows in knowing salute, nodding with his own mouth full, as though this were one of the less mysterious things about food.

His shaded garden he irrigated with water from an artesian well. The water tasted slightly of cedars and made me think of the lush, humid fragrance of hot-houses. In addition to vegetables growing there he had several peach trees and ten or twelve rosebushes.

I was there all afternoon. We spoke a little of domestic plants, and the tinkling notes of black-throated sparrows in his garden, but there were long moments of silence.

In the evening he fixed a stew of jackrabbit and quail. When I asked, he said he caught them in snares made from strippings from mesquite roots. Had he known the Pima who had lived here, or read the work of Gibson and Santander? Or ever seen Harrington, who learned to speak the Pima language but whose extensive field notes lie buried and unread? No, he said, he knew little in this area: his interests outside reading and tending his garden were only mathematical puzzles and playing a clavichord that stood in the room. I didn't know what to expect from the instrument; when he played it later that evening he imparted a sweetness, a fragility to the notes that evoked poignant memories.

Though he was not talkative he did not seem to mind my asking questions. I remember thinking of him that evening as a large bird like a night heron, who might rise and glide away through one of the windows and out across the valley.

I asked about his family, where were they from? Up from Sonora, now scattered. I asked about his education. Through the early grades in Nogales and Tucson, several years in college in Flagstaff, then only reading. I asked about his work. He had had many jobs, moving around Arizona and New Mexico, the Imperial Valley in California, until he was in his forties. In 1958 his grandfather died, bequeathing him the land and a small inheritance. He worked in Steadman now when he needed money.

I became slightly anxious at twilight, not being sure of the way back to the car, and having come to realize that I had perhaps asked too many questions.

We sat in silence for a time. He read. I listened to the air moving through the trees outside. The air was so dry it barely held the fragrance of his garden; only the roses, faintly, if one went to the window and inhaled. I was reminded again of my boyhood in doing this, for there had always been flowers present in the house, especially camellias.

He played something I did not know on the clavichord, which he said was Bach's *First Partita*, and a few pieces by Eric Satie, one called *Trois Avant-dernières Pensées*, and then he made fresh coffee, very dark and thick. He asked me where I was from, and of my life. I was surprised to find myself so at ease. I answered him simply, without elaboration. He was interested in my father. I told him about coming to the valley with him to look for a kind of cactus. When I described it he seemed amused by the idea of its discovery. He had used it to treat depression, he said, making an ablution from its juice and fiber to rub over his hands, which he then allowed to dry in the air. Was he often depressed? I asked. He answered by indicating the landscape beyond, as though the answer were self-evident, one growing out of the other, no more to be avoided than cactus spines or the rocks under one's feet. "Only once in a great while," he said.

I wanted to ask him about the coffee, how he had managed to keep it so fresh. Did he buy only a little and use it up right away? He smiled as if the question pleased him. As one grew older, he said, one learned that with enough care almost anything would keep. It was only a matter of choosing what to take care of. "I have taken great care of a very old instrument," he said. "Come and see."

In the corner of the other room in the house, where his books filled the walls, was an orrery. It looked at first like a standing globe but was a compact set of inset spheres and geared wheels that drove planets and their moons around a central sun. Another clockwork mechanism linked the planets with their satellites, so that they moved relative to each other in imitation of the movements of the solar system. The machine was made of iron, bright brass, and a dark oiled wood like mahogany. There was about it something powerful and immediate.

I could barely step forward to touch it. He waved me closer impatiently, both acknowledging my awe and dismissing it with the same gesture. He put my hands on its parts and I stood transfixed as he demonstrated the intricacies of its movements. Mercury turning inside Venus; Ganymede, the largest moon of Jupiter, turning with Io and the others around its mother planet; and beyond Saturn nothing—Uranus, Neptune, Pluto all undiscovered. As he explained its history and the mathematical relationships of its parts he spoke of celestial winds—and I asked at that moment if the winds in the valley seemed peculiar to him, celestial or even otherworldly? Yes, he answered, as though this were the very point he wished to make. Yes, they did.

He stepped out into the garden, into the bright November evening, and I followed as he led through brittle brush where I was afraid of stepping on rattlesnakes. After a few minutes we came to the open area I recognized as the place where I had first seen him. The wind was just noticeable to me then, but it was evidently blowing hard enough at a distance to disturb some of the stones set down on the cleared plain. He motioned for me to keep my place and went on. I could see by his clothing as he moved away that he was walking into hurricane winds, that they snapped all around him, though I could still feel only a slight breeze and hear no sounds.

He moved several stones, seemed to orient himself, and amid spurts of dust I saw the stones lift off the ground. As they rose from the earth, they began to move in an arc across the sky, turning finally overhead in a dark shape like a pinwheel, some four or five hundred yards across. Now there was a waterfall sound, but only the lightest feeling of a breeze against my cheeks. The man came toward me, acknowledging my dumbstruck stare with a conspiratorial nod that indicated he thought it was impressive too. Perhaps because of friction, each of the thousands of stones now glowed, and they assumed the shape of a galaxy against the dark blue sky, like a bloom of phosphor rolling over in the night ocean.

"The winds," he said, "they are like nothing else in the valley. They stand fully revealed from the moment you first see them. I threw up a handful of petals from the rosebushes. In return—this. I just had to find rocks and stones the right size, make the initial arrangement, Alpha Centauri here, stars of Boötes over there, Cassiopeia on the other side. I noticed the winds immediately—really, I think it was nothing more than throwing up rose petals summer mornings, and they blow like this. Of course, the winds here were unusual to begin with."

"Yes," I said.

He pointed to a spot where the planets around our own sun were visible.

"This is beyond—I can't believe this," I said.

"Yes," he said. "Yes, I know."

The galaxy turned slowly above us. I stood with my hands holding the top of my head, the tail of my shirt lifting slightly in the breeze.

"If one is patient," he said, "if you are careful, I think there is probably nothing that cannot be retrieved."

Winter Count 1973: Geese, They Flew Over in a Storm

H E followed the bellboy off the elevator, through a foyer with forlorn leather couches, noting how low the ceiling was, with its white plaster flowers in bas-relief —and that there were no windows. He followed him down a long corridor dank with an air of fugitives, past dark, impenetrable doors. At the distant end of the next corridor he saw gray thunderheads and the black ironwork of a fire escape. The boy slowed down and reached out to slide a thick key into the lock and he heard the sudden alignment of steel tumblers and their ratchet click. The door swung open and the boy entered, with the suitcase bouncing against the crook at the back of his knee.

He tipped the boy, having no idea what amount was now thought proper. The boy departed, leaving the room sealed off as if in a vacuum. The key with the ornate brass fob lay on a glass table. The man stood by the bed with his hands folded at his lips as though in prayer. Slowly he cleared away the drapes, the curtains and the blinds and stared out at the bare sky. Wind whipped rain in streaks across the glass. He had never been to New Orleans. It was a vague streamer blowing in his memory, like a boyhood acquaintance with Lafcadio Hearn. Natchez Trace. Did Choctaw live here? he wondered. Or Chitamacha? Before them, worshippers of the sun.

He knew the plains better. Best. The high plains north of the Platte River.

He took off his shoes and lay on the bed. He was glad for the feel of the candlewick bedspread. Or was it chenille? He had had this kind of spread on his bed when he was a child. He removed his glasses and pinched the bridge of his nose. In all these years he had delivered so few papers, had come to enjoy much more listening to them, to the stories unfolding in them. It did not matter to him that the arguments were so abstruse they were all but impregnable, that the thought in them would turn to vapor, an arrested breath. He came to hear a story unfold, to regard its shape and effect. He thought one unpacked history, that it came like pemmican in a parfleche and was to be consumed in a hard winter.

The wind sucked at the windows and released them suddenly to rattle in their metal frames. It made him think of home, of the Sand Hills. He lay motionless on the bed and thought of the wind. Crow men racing naked in an April rain, with their hair, five-foot-long black banners, spiraling behind, splashing on the mus-cled rumps of white horses with brown ears.

> 1847 One man alone defended the Hat in a fight with the Crow
>
> 1847 White buffalo, Dusk killed it
>
> 1847 Daughter of Turtle Head, her clothes caught fire and she was burned up
>
> 1847 Three men who were women came

He got up and went to his bag. He took out three stout willow sticks and bound them as a tripod. From its apex he hung a beaded bag of white elk hide with long fringe. The fringe was wrinkled from having been folded against itself in his suit pocket.

> 1891 Medicine bundles, police tore them open

What did they want from him? A teacher. He taught, he did not write papers. He told the story of people coming up from the Tigris-Euphrates, starting there. Other years he would start in a different place—Olduvai, Afar Valley. Or in Tierra del Fuego with the Onas. He could as easily start in the First World of the Navajo. The point, he told his students, was not this. There was no point. It was a slab of meat. It was a rhythm to dance to. It was a cloak that cut the wind when it blew hard enough to crack your soul.

1859 Ravens froze, fell over

1804 Heavy spring snow. Even the dogs went snow-blind

He slept. In his rumpled suit. In the flat, reflected storm light his face appeared ironed smooth. The wind fell away from the building and he dreamed.

For a moment he was lost. Starlight Room. Tarpon Room. Oak Room. He was due—he thought suddenly of aging, of illness: *when our children, they had strangulations of the throat,* of the cure for *any* illness as he scanned the long program—in the Creole Room. He was due in the Creole Room. Roger Callahan, Nebraska State College: "Winter Counts from the Dakota, the Crow and the Blackfeet: Personal Histories."

Jesus, he thought, why had he come? He had been asked. They had asked.

"Aha, Roger."

"I'm on time? I got—"

"You come right this way. I want you in front here. Everyone is very excited, very excited, you know. We're very glad you came. And how is Margaret?"

"Yes—. Margaret died. She died two years ago."

1837 Straight Calf took six horses from the Crow and gave them to Blue Cloud Woman's father and took her

1875 White Hair, he was killed in a river by an Omaha man

1943 John Badger Heart killed in an automobile crash

He did not hear the man. He sat. The histories began to cover him over like willows, thick as creek willows, and he reached out to steady himself in the pool of time.

He listened patiently to the other papers. Edward Rice Phillips, Purdue: "The Okipa Ceremony and Mandan Sexual Habits." The Mandan, he thought, they were all dead. Who would defend them? Renata Morrison, University of Texas: "The Role of Women in Northern Plains Religious Ceremonials."

1818 Sparrow Woman promised the Sun
     Dance in winter if the Cree didn't find us

1872 Comes Out of the Water, she ran off the
     Assiniboine horses

1904 Moving Gently, his sister hung herself

He tried to listen, but the words fell away like tumbled leaves. Cottonwoods. Winters so bad they would have to cut down cottonwood trees for the horses to eat. *So cold we got water from beaver holes only.* And years when they had to eat the horses. *We killed our ponies and ate them. No buffalo.*

Inside the windowless room (he could not remember which floor the elevator had opened on) everyone was seated in long rows. From the first row he could not see anyone. He shifted in his seat and his leather bag fell with a slap against the linoleum floor. How long had he been carrying papers from one place to another like this? He remembered a friend's poem about a snowy owl dead behind glass in a museum, no more to soar, to hunch and spread his wings and tail and fall silent as moonlight.

1809 Blue feathers found on the ground from
     unknown birds

1811 Weasel Sits Down came into camp with
     blue feathers tied in his hair

There was distant applause, like dry brush rattling in the wind.

Years before, defense of theory had concerned him. Not now. "I've thrown away everything that is no good," he told a colleague one summer afternoon on his porch, as though shouting over the roar of a storm. "I can no longer think of anything worse than proving you are right." He took what was left and he went on from there.

> 1851 No meat in camp. A man went to look for buffalo and was killed by two Arapaho
>
> 1854 The year they dragged the Arapaho's head through camp

". . . and my purpose in aligning these four examples is to clearly demonstrate an irrefutable, or what I consider an irrefutable, relationship: the Arikara never . . ."

When he was a boy his father had taken him one April morning to watch whooping cranes on estuaries of the Platte, headed for Alberta. The morning was crucial in the unfolding of his own life.

> 1916 My father drives east for hours in silence. We walk out into a field covered all over

with river fog. The cranes, just their legs
are visible

His own count would be personal, more personal,
as though he were the only one.

1918 Father, shot dead. Argonne forest

The other years came around him now like soft
velvet noses of horses touching his arms in the dark.
". . . while the Cheyenne, contrary to what Green-
wold has had to say on this point but reinforcing what
has been stated previously by Gregg and Houston,
were more inclined . . ."
He wished for something to hold, something to
touch, to strip leaves barehanded from a chokecherry
branch or to hear rain falling on the surface of a lake.
In this windowless room he ached.

    1833 Stars blowing around like snow. Some
         fall to the earth

    1856 Reaches into the Enemy's Tipi has a
         dream and can't speak

    1869 Fire Wagon, it comes

Applause.
He stood up and walked in quiet shoes to the stage.

(Once in the middle of class he had stopped to explain his feeling about walking everywhere in silence.) He set his notes on the podium and covered them with his hands. In a clear voice, without apology for his informality or a look at his papers, he unfolded the winter counts of the Sioux warrior Blue Thunder, of the Blackfeet Bad Head, and of the Crow Extends His Paw. He stated that these were personal views of history, sometimes metaphorical, bearing on a larger, tribal history. He spoke of the confusion caused by translators who had tried to force agreement among several winter counts or who mistook mythic time for some other kind of real time. He concluded by urging less contention. "As professional historians, we have too often subordinated one system to another and forgotten all together the individual view, the poetic view, which is as close to the truth as the consensus. Or it can be as distant."

He felt the necklace of hawk talons pressing against his clavicles under the weight of his shirt.

The applause was respectful, thin, distracted. As he stepped away from the podium he realized it was perhaps foolish to have accepted the invitation. He could no longer make a final point. He had long ago lost touch with the definitive, the awful distance of reason. He wanted to go back to the podium. You can only tell the story as it was given to you, he wanted to say. Do not lie. Do not make it up.

He hesitated for a moment at the edge of the stage. He wished he were back in Nebraska with his students, to warn them: it is too dangerous for everyone to have the same story. The same things do not happen to everyone.

He passed through the murmuring crowd, through a steel fire door, down a hallway, up a flight of stairs, another, and emerged into palms in the lobby.

> 1823 A man, he was called Fifteen Horses, who was heyoka, a contrary, sacred clown, ran at the Crow backwards, shooting arrows at his own people. The Crow shot him in midair like a quail. He couldn't fool them

He felt the edge of self-pity, standing before a plate-glass window as wide as the spread of his arms and as tall as his house. He watched the storm that still raged, which he could not hear, which he had not been able to hear, bend trees to breaking, slash the surface of Lake Pontchartrain and raise air boiling over the gulf beyond. "Everything is held together with stories," he thought. "That is all that is holding us together, stories and compassion."

He turned quickly from the cold glass and went up in the silent elevator and ordered dinner. When it came, he threw back the drapes and curtains and opened the windows. The storm howled through his room and roared through his head. He breathed the wet air deep into his lungs. In the deepest distance, once, he heard the barking-dog sounds of geese, running like horses before a prairie thunderstorm.

The Tapestry

MY FATHER grew up in the north of Spain, in a fishing village in Asturias called Cudillero. He moved later to the south of England, then to America. As he grew older he lost his desire to travel alone and asked me to accompany him. We always went to Spain together. I met members of his family who still lived in Asturias and came to know better his relatives in Madrid. I still thought of them as his relatives rather than my own, for they remained distant and unfamiliar to me, even after I met them. They had opposed his marriage to my mother, I understood.

Europe changed for me during those visits. It became somber and melancholic. Or perhaps I only grew
older and more serious, and now memory seeks some
end of its own. Europe drew me powerfully when I was
younger. When I graduated from high school, the
product of a rigorous Jesuit education, I was awed by
European culture, and impressionable. I went there
immediately after graduation with several classmates
and did things anyone could have predicted. Not wanting to be taken for an American, I spoke only French.
I learned to prefer espresso. I even affected what
seemed to me a European habit—tearing, rather than
biting, pieces off my dinner roll. For three months I
rose each day at dawn and went out, not wanting to
miss any part of the day. I walked about nearly overwhelmed by the opportunity before me. I put off going
to the bars at night; the sensual experiences I wanted
were with the things that had become metaphorical fix-
tures in my mind. The gardens at Versailles, because of
their contrived but soothing order. I wanted to see As-
sisi, the high Gothic cathedral at Rheims, Bosch's *Garden of Delights,* and Newton's rooms at Cambridge.

In that superficial but harmless way of boys of seventeen, I decided that summer that Christopher Wren
was not highly enough regarded, that Mann was correct—something evil did lurk in Venice—and that the
paintings of the Prado far surpassed those in the
Louvre. This all passed in time, though some of these

judgments proved to have a certain foundation and were long-lived. On subsequent trips I often visited the Prado. I spent long hours standing among the Rubenses, the Velazquezes and Goyas and Grecos. It is by such early, seemingly inconsequential and innocent passions, of course, that we are formed.

The spring after my father's death I went to Madrid to close out his affairs, and, as seemed proper, stayed with his relatives. One evening, a dinner guest who had known my father from Cudillero, Eugenio Piera, invited me to visit the Prado where he was a curator. I hesitated to accept, wary of a guided tour, however well intentioned. Museums were places of intense, private feeling for me. But I accepted Piera's invitation. He was genial; he seemed sincere and kindly disposed. We arranged to meet in his office in the basement of the museum the following day.

The next morning I walked the several miles from the apartment down the Paseo de la Castellana, had coffee and croissants in one of the open cafes, and was glad again I had come in April. The air was cool, the trees in leaf, well-dressed people were walking about. The order, the endurance of Spain, soothed me now.

I met Piera at his office. He put me immediately at ease and I felt a twinge of embarrassment at having vaguely mistaken his warmth for acquisitiveness the day before, as one can do in the wake of death. We spent most of the morning in the galleries of the main floor. He told wonderful, arcane stories about some of the acquisitions, was self-deprecating about the petty jealousies of museum collectors, and tried with anecdotes to make the artists more real and fallible. He made serious points, too, but not in a heavy-handed way.

We ate lunch at a nearby restaurant, Las Puertas. He asked if perhaps on another visit to the museum I had seen a fifteenth-century Flemish tapestry that had once hung in my grandfather's house in Cudillero. I had not. But of all the members of my father's family I felt closest to my grandfather, whom I had never met; I was immediately interested.

"How did it come to be in the museum?"

"Your uncle, Ramirez. He got it when your grandfather died. It's unusual, I think, haunting, more like Bruegel or Bosch. It's a very good piece."

The tapestry hung in a storage room. I expected it to have an effect on me right away, but it didn't. It was large, eighteen feet by twelve, depicting scenes of rustic and courtly life separated slightly from each other by a pattern of tiny, bright flowers.

"One thing," said Piera, "purely a technical detail, is the quality of the cloth. The wool threads in the weft are Arras wool—"

"How did the family come to have it?"

"I don't know, really, but I think your grandfather probably purchased it on a recommendation. He was such an eclectic, you know, a very conscientious buyer but not concerned to be known as a collector. I enjoyed that about him. He was completely unpretentious."

"I've heard these stories. I wish I had known him —he died many years before I was born."

"Oh, yes. You would have liked each other, I think. Well—I wanted you to see this. I thought because of your attraction to the Bosch downstairs this would intrigue you."

"Do you have any papers for it? I had a feeling at lunch that it was very important for me to see this. Now that I am here, I am not so sure—but I feel I am missing something right in front of me. If I had more specific information—"

"Certainly. Of course—I think I understand. This piece is very like your grandfather—please excuse my being so familiar—but, not in the general style or these various scenes, but in the . . . in the innocent brooding that is here. At first,"—his fingers went to the tapestry—"you think it's, I don't know, sinister. But no, nothing you can put your finger on. It's not that. It's brooding, with a foreknowledge of some catastrophe or other. Look, here—at the woman in the garden, and at these men on horseback, the threshing here in the distance. No one is speaking. No one is talking.

They are all staring. But it is still very agreeable. The women are charming, the men handsome, the beautiful scarlet colors, the periwinkles, lilies, daisies—there's no turmoil, but no abandon either. I'll tell you what I think: this is the moment just before the whole scene— all these people, the castle, the town, the countryside— is destroyed, and they know it. Do you know what St. Ignacio said, knowing the end of the world, what would you do? Would you run to the confessional? No! he said. You go on doing whatever you are doing. This tapestry reminds me of that detachment from, I don't know—terror. Your grandfather was like that—serene, ingenuous, but still aware of a tremendous evil in the world."

Piera's fingers touched several of the scenes of women sewing, of men in pursuit of a hart. He looked across the tapestry as a man might examine a wall he has just painted, to see if he's missed any parts.

"I'm very fond of this piece, but I can't tell you why. What a thing for a curator to say, eh?" He raised his shoulders in a sign of inexplicable confoundment and motioned for me to follow him.

In his office Piera withdrew from his files a set of papers, which he asked his secretary to copy. The man returned in a few minutes with the copies. He had also found a photograph of the tapestry, which he gave me. He gave the papers back to Piera.

I had never felt as close to my grandfather as I did at that moment. The characters of the tapestry, their expressions, all shimmered in my mind—and, too, what Piera had implied, that he had accepted uncertainty in his family and in his daily life, that he was not tyrannized.

I thanked Piera as sincerely as I could, caught for a moment in how differently emotions can be conveyed, wanting to express my gratitude without overstating it. We shook hands impulsively, warmly, hugged a bit sheepishly, and I left. With the documents, the tapestry promised to be much more accessible. I started back quickly to where it hung, intent on fixing all the detail of its texture and proportion and color in my mind, but I was too excited and suddenly afraid of my own compulsiveness, that I was making a mistake. I continued downstairs, out through the rotunda and into the street, intending to come back.

I walked for miles in a state of both consternation and ease, unwilling to focus my conscious thoughts for fear of closing off something much deeper. I saw the emotional abyss in which I had placed both my father and grandfather. Piera's belief that my grandfather was aware of a tremendous evil—it had been years since I had dwelled on what was evil.

By the time I stopped walking I was in an unfamiliar section of the city. I sat down in a small park for a while, watching the faces pass, and then crossed the street to a cafe, believing coffee would induce an order from which I could proceed.

I took the papers Piera had given me out of my

pocket and began to read. The artist was unknown, but the design was probably from one by Jennyn Fabiaen of Bruges. Woven *c.* 1485, perhaps in Tournai. The information that followed—the French family who had commissioned the tapestry, their contributions to the arts—all this drew me away from what I sought. I recalled how sensitive the portrayal of the hands had been, the silent eyes, the bright translucent air—". . . the change from almost white highlights to the deepest purple is managed with only three transitional shades. The resulting effect is a miracle of harmony and relief." I looked quickly at the last page—technical notes. The scarlet reds were "derived from the crushed bodies of cochineal insects from the New World"; silk thread was used "for details such as the women's hair and the line of the horizon, which require more refined execution."

I sipped my coffee and looked up at a wind cutting into the crowns of plane trees in the little park. Calmer now, I went carefully over each page of what Piera had given me, following the descriptions on the photograph with my finger, the references to historical figures and the symbols in each scene. There were hundreds of historical details—a famous horse, a heraldic forgery, the words of a love ballad cleverly hidden in a huntsman's banner. But in the end the details did not touch each other. The vision, insight into my grandfather that I sought, was now very distant. My understanding of the black-and-white photograph, the tapestry itself, the faces, all of it had shifted. In the quiet slanting light of late afternoon I felt foolish.

I put several coins on the table and left.

"Senor! Ud. ha olvidado esto," called the waiter, holding up the papers and photograph.

"No. No son mios, eso es de otra persona." They belong to someone else. I strode up the avenue feeling tight in my throat but with a feeling of sudden release, of guarded elation. I felt rid of a daunting exhortation to examine life which had hung in the air since my father's death. I wanted very much to feel what I had felt as a boy walking out of the confessional, the moral debris swept away, all extenuating circumstances dismissed. That absolution was irrevocable. You could go ahead certain in the knowledge. I had each step before me again, if I wished; between myself and my father, and a grandfather whom I could only imagine. I could feel the nearness of tears, those that threaten when one senses how much one wants a promise of intimacy to be real.

In death, both the strange elation and the withering sadness arrive simultaneously. One day, I thought, they wind themselves back together and disappear.

The sun was awash now, fiery on the Manzanares River. I thought that I would ask my relatives about my grandfather's attitude toward his enemies. It would

be possible to start there. Then I would go back to the
Prado and see the tapestry and Piera again. And then I
would go home. The sun is setting at this moment
across the harbor at Cudillero. I could go there, and
sail home from La Coruña.

The Woman
Who Had Shells

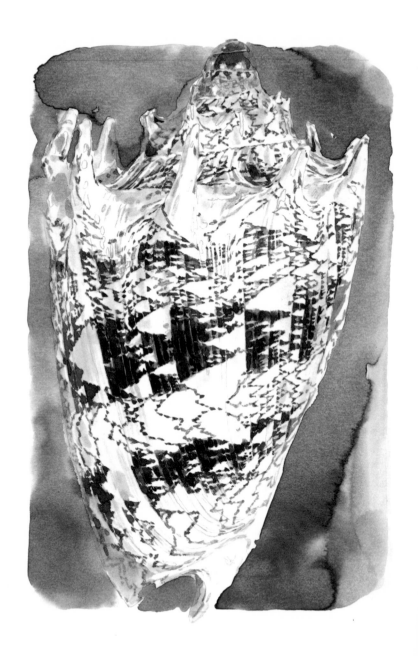

THE LIGHT is blinding. The vast, flat beaches of Sanibel caught in the Caribbean noon are fired with a white belligerence, shells lying in such profusion that people unfamiliar arrive believing no one has ever been here. The shells draw July heat from the languid air, shells brittle as Belleek, hard as stove bolts, with blushing, fluted embouchures, a gamut of watercolor pinks and blues. Shivering iridescence rises from abalone nacre. Hieroglyphics climb the walls of slender cones in spiraling brown lines. Conchs have the heft of stones. One shell hides both fists; others could be swallowed without discomfort, like pills. A form of genuflection turned over in the hand becomes a form of containment, its thin pastels the colors to chalk a prairie sunrise.

Here at dusk one afternoon, thinking I was alone, I took off a pair of pants, a light shirt, my shoes and shorts and lay down. On my back, arms outstretched, I probed the moist, cool surfaces beneath the sheet of white shells still holding the day's heat. I flexed and shifted against them until I lay half buried, as if floating in saltwater. The afternoon trailed from me. I was aware of a wisp of noise, like a waterfall muffled in deep woods. The pulse of my own heart faded and this sound magnified until in the mouths of the thousands of shells around and beneath me it became a wailing, a keening as disarming, as real, as sudden high winds at sea. It was into this moment—I remember opening my eyes suddenly to see flamingos overhead, their lugubrious flight etched against a lapis sky by the last shafts of light, the murmuring glow of pale crimson in their feathered bellies—into this moment that the woman stepped.

I turned my head to the side, ear pressed into the shells, and saw her first at a great distance. I was drawn to her immediately, to her tentative, cranelike movements, the reach of her hand. I imagined her fingers as polite as the waters of a slow and shallow creek, searching, sensitive even to the colors of shells, the trace of spirits. She was nearer now. With one movement she bent down and raised two shells, scallops, and cupped them to her cheeks. I saw clear in her face a look I have seen before only in the face of a friend who paints, when he has finished, when the mystery is established and accepted without explanation. I held that connection in my mind even as she turned away, knowing the chance these emotions were the same was only slight, so utterly different are human feelings, but believing we could, and do, live by such contrivance.

I wanted to speak out but could not move. She grew smaller, touched one or two more places on the beach, like an albatross trying to alight against a wind, took nothing and disappeared.

I stared across the white expanse into the vault of the evening sky, toward the emergence of the first stars. My respect for her was without reason and profound. I lay for hours unable to move. Whenever the urge to rise and dress welled up, a sense of the density of the air, of one thought slipping irretrievably off another into darkness overwhelmed me. When finally I stood, I saw fields of shells around me luminescent in the starlight. Near where my head had been was a single flamingo feather. Across this landscape I made my way home.

We carry such people with us in an imaginary way, proof against some undefined but irrefutable darkness in the world. The nimbus of that moment remained with me for months. That winter, on a beach frozen to stone I stood staring at the pack ice of the Arctic Ocean. The gray sea ice gave way to gray sky in such a way that no horizon could be found. In the feeble light my breath rolled out, crystallized I knew on my eyebrows, on the fur at the edge of my face. I wanted a memento. With my heel I began to chip at the thin, wind-crusted snow on the sand. There was a small shell, a blue and black mussel barely the length of my fingernail. Stiff with the cold, I was able only with great difficulty to maneuver it into a pocket of my parka, and to zip it shut. I was dimly aware at that moment of the woman, the turning of her skirt, extending her hand to the shells on Sanibel Island.

In one of the uncanny accidents by which life is shaped, I saw the woman the following year in New York. It was late in winter. I saw her through a window, reaching for her water glass in a restaurant on West 4th Street, that movement.

It was early in the evening, hardly anyone there. I crossed the room and asked if I might sit down. She did not move. The expression in her face was unreadable. I recounted, as respectful of her privacy as I could be, how I had first seen her. She smiled and nodded acquiescence. For a moment I was not sure it was the same woman. She seemed veiled and unassuming.

She was a photographer, she said. She had been

photographing in St. Petersburg when she went out that afternoon to Sanibel. I had been on vacation, I told her; I taught Asian history at the University of Washington—we found a common ground in Japan. A collection of her photographs of farms and rural life on the most northern island, Hokkaido, had just been published. I knew the book. In memory I saw images of cattle grazing in a swirling snowstorm, a weathered cart filled with a dimpled mound of grain, and birdlike hands gripping tools. In those first moments the images seemed a logical and graceful extension of her.

We talked for hours—about bumblebees and Cartier-Bresson, haiku, Tibet, and Western novels; and I asked if I could see her home. There was by then a warmth between us, but I could sense the edges of her privacy and would rather say good night, seal the evening here, hold that memory, than burden either of us. There is so much unfathomable in human beings; we so often intrude, meaning no harm, and injure for no reason. No, she said, she wouldn't mind at all.

We walked a great many blocks north, then east toward the river. There was ice on the sidewalks and we linked arms against it. Her apartment was a flat above weathered storefronts. We sat on a couch in a spacious room painted white, softly lit, with several large photographs on the wall, of seagrass and of trees in a field in Michigan. I had thought there would be shells somewhere in the room, but there were not that I saw.

I began looking through one of her published books, black-and-white photographs of rural Maine. She fixed a gentle tea, like camomile. We sipped tea. She was very quiet and then she spoke about the shells. Whenever there was time, she said, she went out looking. When she was in Australia to work or in the Philippines, or on the coast of Spain. When she first began she would collect them. Now it was rare that she ever brought one home, even though she continued to search, hoping especially to see a hypatian murex and other shells that she might never find, or find and leave. When she took vacations she used to go alone to exotic beaches on the Coral and South China seas, and to places like the Seychelles. Then, more and more, she stayed home, going to Block Island or Martha's Vineyard, to Assateague Island or to Padre Island in Texas, spending days looking at the simplest whelks and clams, noting how very subtly different they all were. The day I had seen her, she said, was one of the times she had gone to Sanibel to walk, to pick up a shell, turn it in the white tropical light, feel the cusps and lines, and set it back. As she described what she saw in the shells she seemed slowly to unfold. The movement of her hands to her teacup now had the same air of reticence, of holy retrieval and graceful placement that I had seen that day. She spoke of limpid waters, of unexpected colors, mikado yellow, cerulean blue, crimson flush, of their baroque and simple structure, their strength and fragility. Her voice was intimate, almost plaintive. When she stopped speaking it was very still.

The first pearling of light was visible on the window panes. After a long moment I walked quietly to where my coat lay and from a pocket took the small mussel shell from the Arctic coast. I returned to her. I said in the most subdued voice I could find where the shell had come from, and what it meant because of that day on Sanibel Island, and that I wished her to have it. She took it. What was now in the room I had no wish to disturb.

I crossed the room again to get my coat. She followed. At the door where I thought to try to speak there was a gentle pressure on my arm and she led me to the room where she slept. Her bed was on the floor. Two windows looked east over the city. By the bed was a small white table with a glass top set over what had once been a type drawer. In its compartments were shells.

She slid back the sheet of glass and sitting there on her heels she began to show them to me. In response to a question, she would say where a shell was from or the circumstances under which she had found it. Some were so thin I could see the color of my skin through them. Others were so delicately tinged I had to be told their color. They felt like bone, like water-worn glass and raw silk. Patterns like African fabric and inscriptions of Chinese characters. Cone shells like Ming vases. She turned my hand palm up and deposited in its depression what I at first thought were grains of sand. As my eye became accustomed to them I saw they were shells, that each one bore in infinitesimal precision a sunburst of fluting. The last she lay in my hands was like an egg, as white as alabaster and as smooth, save that its back was so intricately carved that my eye foundered in the detail.

She put the shells back and carefully replaced the glass. There was a kind of silence in the room that arrives only at dawn. Light broke the edge of a building and entered the window, bringing a glow to the pale curve of her neck. In the wall steam pipes suddenly hammered. Her hair moved, as if in response to breath, and I saw the flush outline of her cheek. In that stillness I heard her step among the shells at Sanibel and heard the pounding of wings overhead and imagined it was possible to let go of a fundamental anguish.

The Lover of Words

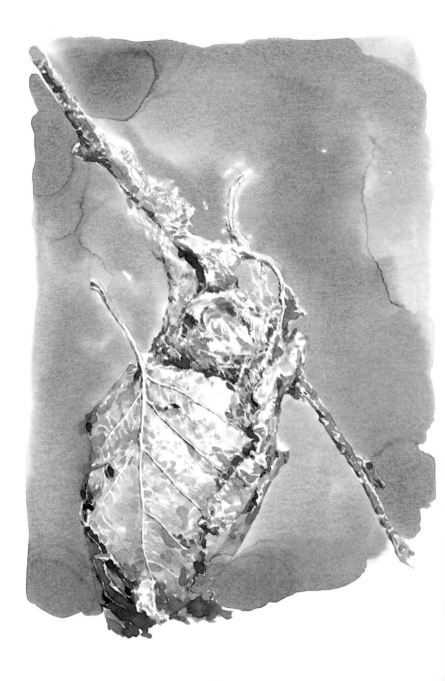

YOU MUST understand something the other way around first: he was a common gardener. He was Mexican and he lived in the barrio of East Los Angeles, and though his profession came to him inexorably, father to son, his awareness of a world apart from his menial labors was both sublime and pervasive. He was a reader of fictions, in English and Spanish. He was thirty-one, unmarried, diffident, and preoccupied with words, not as a linguist might be but only as an autodidact would be: he understood the power of words to draw forth feeling and to mesmerize. He understood how words healed.

He did not conceive his existence, as a well-read man whose sense of affluence came as easily from an encounter with a felicitous phrase as it did among roses, as anomalous, for his perceptions were not directed that way. Nothing in his own mind told him his life was either eccentric or incongruous; he was not aware that the idea of his existence was clichéd. So whatever objection there was to him—haughty regard in a clerk who waited with him at a bus stop while he read *The Autumn of the Patriarch*—took place beyond him. He was astute enough to have developed a hedgerow, pleasant as lilacs, that separated him from engaging conversation with employers and most Anglos. But he did not apprehend it as a barrier, for he had no inclination to dwell on contrivance in life, or the reasons for it. He was in touch with subtle currents only to preserve an undisturbed life.

Several things were important to him. He did not wish to lead an eleemosynary existence. He did not wish to be distracted from ritual, either from the cultivation of plants in the shaded gardens of Beverly Hills or from sequence in a life of readings, whereby one book leads by diaphanous but ineluctable threads to the next. But these were not ideas in his mind; he was as ingenuous with himself as he was with everyone he met. And preternaturally quiet; there was a haunting quietude both inside and outside him, and in the penumbra of this order one might have expected wild beasts to be as tractable as daffodils.

He was not unaware; he accepted the servitude and the iniquity of his position apart from the living of his life. He understood racism, but his spirit was not crushed by it. He had found, in the same way a tree sends its roots down in search of water and its limbs to find light, a plane of alignment, and he was partly invisible in it. He nourished himself with words and he took another kind of sustenance, as necessary, from daily contact with the soil.

He had found, by a subterranean and labyrinthine route, some way around hatred, too, so that his anger in the face of cravenness and savagery was no less, but he was not obsessed with revenge or rectitude. He slept deeply; he read at dawn in a quality of light that moved him on occasion as deeply as the words in his lap. Yet he was not conscious of escape.

He appreciated the quality and design of his tools and was solicitous after them. He was expert in the repair of machinery. And he wrote poetry in the evening, against a breeze from the window. It was not brilliant poetry, for he could not effect the transition from what he admired to what he wrote, but this did not come into his mind. The lines were not insipid or the emotions exaggerated. He tended to them with the same care with which he gardened, but not the same industry, and here lay his sense of humor, and balance.

He knew several women, with whom he sometimes spent the night and in whose company he would almost emerge from the chrysalis of his life. He was not bothered by thoughts of loneliness or wasted time or ambitionless existence or any of the other pronouncements made more on his life than to his person by his employers. He was in their view only a peculiar and ingratiating Mexican, to be impugned as one would speak distractedly of the weather.

As long as he was at a remove from such people he was untouched by their condescension and presumption; and he attended carefully to this remove.

At an all-but-unfathomable depth in his spirit, however, there lay an irreducible idea, medieval and adamantine, about the replicating quality of metaphor and the physical revelation of abstract ideas. As he tended to his bushes and plants, to the trimming of lawns and hillsides of ivy, he drew himself along in a world of cultivated ideas, trimmed and watered as expeditiously, from which arose an atmosphere as salubrious.

As a stone waits millennia to trip a certain horse on a well-worn path, so now did this convergence between ideas and work begin to take shape in his mind, to cross over a threshold, become real, and occupy him.

One day, his brown arms girdling a load of palm fronds, he paused mid-step, as if trying to remember something, aware of the sweep of ineffable evening color behind him, and grasped a passing vision of destruction. He walked up the hill thinking of tulip bulbs.

The unraveling of himself was like the retreat of a tide, an undeniable movement but not apparent at any particular moment. Only with reference to the same points could he be sure of the change. He found himself wishing his poetry were more accomplished; he ruminated while he worked about the rudeness and unexamined prejudice of the children of his employers. He found cupidity in himself, and became aware of a vague resentment toward his surroundings. He developed a mean-spirited attitude toward what he read and realized he had a capacity for smugness. He had never, in all his life, been so aware of himself. And he suspected it was this preoccupation that began to exacerbate so severely a sense of drowning.

Once outside himself and thus an observer he became lost. Each of his actions took on such metaphysical weight he was hamstrung by the simplest tasks. Trimming rosebushes, once a graceful movement with him, was now a desultory and inefficient feint. The mechanical exigencies of lawnmowers defeated him. Food lost its taste. He stopped reading.

The more he thought, the more unhinged he became, until finally he believed he must speak with someone. Of the women he knew, only one could help, and all she could do was offer him her belief in his spirit, and it was not enough for him.

No one, he realized, could understand the unfolding of his predicament because he had not taken anyone in.

He thought to arrest his downward movement—which baffled and angered him because it proceeded without reason, and he had become too acutely aware of the role of reason in people's lives—by discipline. He set back to reading. He allotted a certain number of books to read each week. Words he did not know he made lists of, so he would be sure to look them up. His therapeutic attempt to reclaim his self-possessed and undisturbed self was mirrored for him in the gardens he tended; he made judgments on his state and wondered at his progress by studying the movements of his hands among the flowers. How deft? he would ask himself. How portentous? he would ask, and so continue in his own self-destruction.

One afternoon he was cogitating over a word he had encountered that morning and become enamored of immediately because it was a word he felt caught for a moment in its definition the meaning of his condition: sharawadji, a graceful disorder. As one fans a deck of cards he fanned this notion in his mind until in the farrago of ideas he saw himself as metaphysically disheveled but still presentable (even more conscious now of being Mexican), and saw as well the irony of neat gardens, deeply rooted, surrounding the houses of superficial people in moral disarray (thus did he tap his own bigotry). On another day, after he had entered a period of self-pity, he dwelled on the word ahimsa, the doctrine of respect for all living things. And thus did he develop scruples about the rights of aphids and the crying of mown grass. And one evening after work, taking a chance that would not have occurred to him a month before, he entered a guest house and with his list of words began paging through a large dictionary which lay inert on a wrought-iron floor stand. The owner stepped in on him; he was apologetic and properly obsequious, but it was clear almost immediately that something else was required. He attempted an explanation. His nervousness, his clothing, his accent all undid him; what he hoped would pass for erudition suddenly seemed only stupidity. As he held out the list in desperation he realized it resembled something cribbed and illegal, and he felt the penetration of a sense of injustice. Tact held him to a sense of irony. His rage precipitated only a wry smile.

The loss of other jobs that followed he saw as predictable, a result of the moral and metaphysical overlaying he had indulged. He had never, to his mind, indulged himself before. But he was now bereft of that innocence and he besieged himself with endless mental explanations, and scruples that seemed silly even to him, which made him angrier.

In this state he allowed himself, as it were, to sleep with the devil. He accepted unemployment checks and argued with his neighbors, cursing their Mexican traits and otherwise giving evidence of self-directed anger and, of course, his pain. Concern over the state of his deprivation, the collapse of his virtue and the lassitude that accompanied his depression no longer occupied his mind.

What saved him principally was his belief in physical equivalents, his intuition that under another set of circumstances, contrived but sincere, he could set himself right. For this single reason he went to his father. The father regarded the son as dangerously imaginative and was suspicious of his impenetrable privacy. For years he had thought his son a homosexual. He projected impertinence on him and accused him sharply of cowardice. All this flew over the son as would have the release of so many frantic doves. He sought his father's idea of a place he might go. He explained that he had to get away. He didn't mean to be taken cryptically and was sure after he had said it that his father would interpret the request perversely. Nevertheless, it was a son and a father. His father told him to visit an uncle in Yuma, a clerk in a motel.

The father hugged his son, abruptly but firmly, when he left.

He expected to be gone a while, to find a job, to spend a few weeks in the mountains to the north. He was fortunate in that he took none of these plans seriously; he simply expected to do whatever was necessary to obliterate a sense of himself. The repressed bigotry in Yuma gave him an edge to work against. His uncle went out each evening dressed with a Mexican sense of fastidiousness, and was largely absent. The closeness of the border bred malevolence and suspicion. Tourists wandered the streets as if in a state of forgetfulness. None of this touched him. Only the sense that he was removed from the gardens of Beverly Hills and that he was Mexican and that he enjoyed reading; and certain knowledge that there would be other bends in the river as dangerous for him farther on.

The room in which he stayed took a breeze in the morning. The afternoon light was indirect and seemed to hover in the room. Suddenly one day he was taken with appreciation at the sight of his hard, blunt thumbs against the white pages of a book. The afternoon heat hung in suspension in the air and he felt a delicateness in his belly. He thought of the inscrutable life buried in a wheelbarrow full of bulbs, of the sound of his spade going into the earth, and of his cleverness with water.

He turned pages, and read on.

The Location of
the River

that I got everything wrong

ACCORDING to a journal kept by Benjamin Foster, a historian returning along the Platte River from the deserts of the Great Basin at the time, the spring of 1844 came early to western Nebraska. He recorded the first notes of a horned lark on the sixteenth of February. This unseasonable good weather induced him to stay a few weeks with a band of Pawnee camped just south of the Niobrara River. One morning he volunteered to go out with two men to look for stray horses. They found the horses grazing near an island of oak and ash trees on the prairie, along the edge of the river. When he saw the current and quicksand Foster was glad the horses had not crossed over.

On the way back, writes Foster—little of his last journal survives, but some fragments relevant to this incident are preserved—the Pawnee told him that the previous summer the upper Niobrara had disappeared.

At first Foster took this for a figurative statement about a severe drought, but the other Pawnee told him, no, the Niobrara had not run dry—in fact, the spring of 1843 had been very wet. It disappeared. That Foster took this information seriously, that he did not treat it with skepticism or derision, was characteristic of him.

The Pawnee, he goes on to say, did not associate the disappearance of the river with any one particular phenomenon (Foster, I should say, was a confidant; he spoke fluent Pawnee and I'm sure they felt he was both knowledgeable and trustworthy); they attributed its disappearance to a sort of willful irritation, which they found amusing. They told Foster that the earth, the rivers, did not belong to men but were only to be used by them, and that the earth, though it was pleased with the Pawnee, was very disappointed in the white man. It suited the earth's purpose, they said, to suddenly abandon a river for a while, to confound men who were too dependent on such things always being there.

Foster thought this explanation narrow and self-

serving and told the Pawnee so. But they were ada-
mant. Foster writes that he himself was increasingly at
a loss to understand what had happened, but he had
been among Indians long enough to appreciate their
sense of humor and to know their strength for allegory.
He pointed out to them that if the river had shifted
course or disappeared, the Pawnee would be as affected by it as the white men; but the Pawnee said, no,
this was not so, because they saw things like this all the
time and were not bothered by them.

It is difficult to fathom what happened to the river
or to Foster either, once he concluded, as he apparently did, that the Pawnee were literally correct, that
sometime during the summer of 1843 the upper
reaches of the Niobrara River, above the present town
of Marshland and westward into Wyoming, did vanish
for four or five months.

An initial thought, he wrote, was that the people he
was camped with were not Pawnee. He thought they
might be a little too far north—in Sioux or possibly
Arapaho country. Even though they spoke, ate,
dressed, and even played at sleight-of-hand like Pawnee, they could be somebody else, with a cavalier regard for local truth. In others of his papers Foster
writes about a rite of imitation in which a band of
people from one tribe, Arikara, for example, would
imitate a band from some other tribe for long periods
of time, fifteen years or more. They began doing this

on the northern plains in the 1820s, imitating each other in exacting detail, as a form of amusement. There was no way Foster could be certain he was not among Oglala Sioux pretending to be Pawnee and playing the Long Joke, fooling a white man and making at the same time a joke about their star-gazing neighbors the Pawnee who might not know what was going on at their very feet. But he had been intimate with the Pawnee; after extensive inquiry he believed he was among them, not someone else.

It appears Foster tried systematically to establish a basis for belief in the river's disappearance, and pursued this course with increasing determination, as though he intuited the truth of the thing but didn't know how to demonstrate it. I don't know why, but I feel that, by that point, the man had begun to wonder at all he had seen in his life, and what of any of it would be believed.

The possibility that the river had simply changed its channel seemed plausible to him, but after reconnoitering extensively through the hills he discounted it. And the river had not switched channels or run dry, it was repeatedly emphasized to him, it had vanished. There were no willows on the islands. There were no islands. There were no mud flats, no smooth places even in the sand, no abandoned channels, nothing. With the aid of survey maps made in 1840, and a theodolite, compass, artificial mercury horizon, and other instruments he borrowed from Fort Laramie some hundred miles to the southwest, Foster tried to compare the present location of the river with its location in November 1840, when the maps were made. The disagreements were too insignificant to have meaning, however, what one would have to expect given the crudeness of tools and methods in those days.

Foster subsequently was unable to find any permanent resident to question, or to learn anything from men garrisoned at Fort Laramie or Fort Platte to the south. He rode as far north as the Sioux Agency in South Dakota looking for people to talk to. Exhausting all these traditional methods, he turned finally to something less conventional. It had long been his personal belief (and he was bolstered in this by some of those with whom he lived) that the history of the earth was revealed anew each spring in the shapes of the towering cumulus clouds that moved over the country from the north and west. If a man were blessed, were *wakan*, and had the patience and watched from the time of the first thunderstorm until the first prairie grass fire, he would see it. There was no sequence; the events unfurled in an order of their own, so Foster prepared himself for a long vigil. One April afternoon, seventeen days after he had begun, he saw on the horizon with the aid of an interpreter, as clear as the blades of blue grama grass and his moccasined feet before him, the fading and disappearance of the upper

Niobrara River in the clouds. He judged the time of year to be late June.

This must have been slightly disquieting for Foster, living in two worlds as he did, lying there on his back under the inexorable movement of clouds, feeling the earth turn under him, thinking what he did and did not know, could and could not prove. On the basis of what is a man to be believed?

There is something else here, too. In a letter to Foster dated July 7, 1831, the American explorer and painter George Catlin remarks on his terror of open space in Nebraska. While on foot in the tallgrass prairie, he and his party used a sextant and chronometer, as though at sea. I don't know whether having underlined this passage in Catlin's letter (it survives) means Foster's own perception of the prairie was oceanic—people later spoke of the "coasts of Nebraska"—or whether on his own he had always felt unsettled by the unbounded space, as he might particularly have been that spring.

The disappearance of the upper Niobrara might never have come to light at all had it not been for Foster's breakdown at that point and, much later, the interest of a graduate student at Idaho State University called Anton Breverton. Breverton tried to document Foster's career in the west in his history thesis and he tried especially to clarify this one episode on the Niobrara. I lost touch with Breverton some years ago. He is either living today in obscurity, possibly in Europe, or he has passed on. His thesis, I am sorry to say, is also unavailable. The archival librarian at Pocatello believes his was among some twenty theses lost when the library transferred its collections to a new building in 1948. I read Breverton's thesis at his request when it came out, made a few notes, and returned it. Reconstructing Foster's life had been a preoccupation of mine, too, since coming into possession of the notes and journals he failed to destroy that spring.

Breverton read extensively in the literature of western Nebraska, in science and history, from both native and white sources, trying to find some hint of explanation for the disappearance of the river or what was meant by the Pawnee who told Foster this. He combed emigrants' journals, reports from the Smithsonian, the Carnegie Institution—all fruitless. He even read regional novels, including those of Mari Sandoz, going so far as to go to New York and interview Miss Sandoz. An unusually sensitive woman who grew up in that country at the turn of the century, Sandoz had been particularly attentive to the stories of the region. But Breverton was unable to corroborate any part of it. He finally left it out of his thesis.

I understand a colleague of Breverton, irritated by the entire issue, nearly enraged in fact, secured some military funding to conduct a soil analysis throughout

Dawes, Sioux, and Box Butte counties in Nebraska where the river flows, but I do not know what became of this information. I myself have communicated with the Pawnee Tribal Council, with friends among the Arapaho, and with faculty at the University of Nebraska who could be expected to add something, but to no avail.

For my part, I do not think the river ever disappeared. I imagine Foster, a brilliant man much troubled by the destruction of native cultures, simply fell prey to a final madness.

A catalytic event occurred in Foster's life in 1808 when he was living in a large Chippewa village near the present town of Bayfield, Wisconsin. Representatives of the Shawnee Prophet had come among them and instructed the people to extinguish all their fires, to rekindle fire in the old way with sticks, and to never let it go out. They said the old lifeways would return, that the prophet himself would bring back the dead. The psychologically depressed Chippewa enthusiastically adopted the beliefs of these impassioned young men. A demonstration of allegiance they required was that of throwing away one's personal possessions. As an eleven-year-old boy, Foster saw the shore of Lake Superior lined with the medicine bundles of a thousand men, all washed up by the waves. These small bundles, decorated with trade beads, strips of bright cloth, feathers, and quill work, must have been gathered up by someone (perhaps even Foster) and taken somewhere, for one morning the beaches were empty.

From this time forward, I am sure Foster was possessed of the idea of recording the beliefs of native tribes before they fell victim to whites or to the panic of their own spiritual leaders. This much is clearly implied by a boyhood friend of Foster who wrote about the incident on the lake in *A Narrative of the Captivity and Adventures of John Tanner.* (It is further substantiated in the private papers of W. W. Warren in the manuscript collection of the Minnesota Historical Society. You can appreciate perhaps the difficulty of piecing together Foster's career, in the wake of the destruction of all his notes.)

Foster spent the next thirty years with six or seven different tribes. He is occasionally mentioned in the correspondence of Ogden, Sublette, and others as a translator and Indian expert of exceptional skill. He would apparently live for years with a tribe before moving on. Though loath to do it, he deposited this steady accumulation of field notes periodically at various American and British trading posts for safekeeping, intending one day to collect them all. This is what he was doing in 1844 when he was waylaid by the Pawnee and good weather. He had eleven pack mules with him at the time, all of them burdened with manuscripts. His writings were more detailed, complete, inclusive of fantastic incident, rigorous, and perceptive (to judge from the scraps) than anything Fontenelle,

Maximilian, Ruxton, Stewart, or any of the rest ever wrote down. He was en route to Kansas City, where the great trading family of Chouteau had offered him money for publication. The collection would have equalled in scope and importance the collected volumes on the west edited by Reuben Thwaites some sixty years later. It is one of the great tragedies of American history that he did not arrive and that his manuscripts were ruined.

In late June 1844, after Foster had begun to despair of ever understanding either the fact or the meaning of the disappearance of the river, after a time of ritual cleansing and dreaming, perhaps agoraphobic or maddened by the interweaving of literalisms and metaphors and forms of proof, Foster began throwing his manuscripts into the river. According to a Pawnee called Wolf Finger, who spoke with the historian Henry Lake, Foster would go down naked in the afternoon, wade out into the Niobrara and hurl a fistful of pages into the water, or from the shore he would skip a journal across the surface like a stone. Eventually he threw everything he'd ever written down into the Niobrara River, turned the pack mules out with the Pawnee horses, and left. He went away to the north, "like a surprised grouse whirring off across the prairie."

What was left of these documents came into my hands through my father, a tax assessor. He found them in a barn near Lusk, Wyoming, in 1901. Among them—there was about enough to fill one cardboard box—was the first page of an essay entitled "Studying the Indian." I have no idea of the date. In the first paragraph Foster says, "I have been among the Absarokee when they left the battlefield like sparrows. I have watched Navajo men run down antelope on foot and smother their last breath in a handful of corn pollen. One bad summer in the Desert of the Black Rocks I saw Shoshoni women go out at sunset and because they were starving call in the quail. I have heard the soft syllables of the Arapaho tongue and the choking sound of the Kiowa and the hissing Cheyenne sounds. A woman called Reaches Deep taught me how to dance, and once I danced until I entered the sun. But already in the fall of 1826, in Judith Basin, a Piegan called Coyote in the Camp had told me I was learning everything wrong. . . ." Foster goes on, a few words, the rest is washed out and sun bleached.

In an attempt to understand what little Foster had written down about the disappearance of the Niobrara (and with a sense of compassion for him), I visited that part of the state in 1963. I stayed in a small hotel, the Plainview, in the town of Box Butte. I had with me all of Foster's water-stained notes, which I had spread around the room and was examining again for perhaps the hundredth time. During the night a tremendous rainstorm broke over the prairie. The Niobrara threatened to flood and I was awakened by the motel operator. I drove across the river—in the cone of my headlights I could see the fast brown water surging against the bridge supports—and spent the rest of the night in my car on high ground, at some distance from the town, in some hills the name of which I do not remember. In the morning I became confused on farm roads and was unable to find my way back to the river. In desperation I stopped at a place I recognized having been at the day before and proceeded from there on foot toward the river, until I became lost in the fields themselves. I met a man on a tractor who told me the river had never come over in that direction. Ever. And to get away.

I have not been back in that country since.